KESS

TIJAN

Originally edited and proofread for One More Step anthology by The Bookworm Box.

1

KESS

One more step would mean certain death.

The words were scribbled on a piece of paper, taped to a bathroom stall, and I was about out of patience. I ripped it off, balled it up, and tossed it into the garbage. I knew why they put the note up, because this was the druggie stall.

Asshats.

There were three other stalls open, which wasn't normal, but we were in the end run of the school year. Graduation was in two days. It was our last official day of school, though most seniors stopped coming a long time ago. Not me. I was here because of *detention.*

Detention.

I growled under my breath.

I was about to head inside the stall, find the drugs I knew were stashed somewhere, and I was going to mess with them. I was going to hide them somewhere else in the bathroom, but just as I hit the door to open, the main door to the bathroom swung wide.

In walked Tasmin Shaw.

"Hey, Kess."

I paused, trying to stomp down some of my irritation. It wasn't her fault I was here for detention, but it was her brother's and his whole group's fault. There was a situation they brought about that ended with me getting detention. It was a whole round-about thing, and it didn't really matter in the long run. But, I couldn't be mean to Tasmin Shaw, or Taz as she was called by her friends. There were a few different reasons why I wanted to, but none really had to do with Taz as a person.

One, Taz was nice. Like actually nice.

Two, she was connected. Taz was not only popular, but she was well connected with the toughest crew still going strong in our school. We have a system, or *had* a system. There used to be a whole chain of groups that weren't gangs, but we weren't all friends either. We were in the medium between those extremes, and tended to look down on those who weren't in a crew. That meant you weren't loyal, and if you were crew, loyalty was like blood to us.

You needed it to be crew, or you were simply 'less than.'

Or I used to think so.

And three, there was a respect issue here because Taz's brother's woman was now the *only* female in a crew. There'd been one other girl, but no more, and I can say that because it was me. I used to be in a crew. We weren't big or even tough, but we were a crew and I loved my crew.

Now we were nothing.

"Hey, Taz."

She stopped before going into her own stall, noted where I was standing, and raised her eyebrows. "You okay?"

I'd forgotten what I was going to do.

"Yeah. I'm good."

Taz gave me another smile and went into her stall.

I moved inside mine, and a second later, her voice came through the room. "Do you have any plans for the weekend?"

The weekend. Shit. I usually did, but that was before my crew broke up.

Now, "Not really. You?"

Her toilet flushed—when had she even pissed? A beat later, her door opened, and she went out to the sink. Me, I was still standing just inside my door. I hadn't even closed it behind me, so here we go I guess. I nudged it back open, edging farther out as she washed her hands. Her eyes found mine in the mirror.

An emotion flickered in them, and oh no.

I was already readying myself, because whatever that was, I didn't like it. My gut was tightening up.

"You know, I heard that Zeke Allen from Fallen Crest Academy is probably going to throw a rager. They party almost every night over there."

I wanted to snort in disgust, or at least disdain. I didn't.

"Yeah?"

She nodded, finishing up drying her hands, and stepped back from the sink. "Where are your guys? Usually they'd be out in the hall if you're in here."

There was the whole gut tightening again. Right there.

I jerked a shoulder up. "They're out doing their thing. I'll catch up with them later."

"Are you dating one of them? Monica mentioned that one time."

"Monica doesn't know anything."

She was referring to one of her friends, who truly didn't know shit.

"Oh."

Those eyes of hers. Tawny and hazel, and there's a reason she and her brother were some of the most ridiculously good-looking people in our school. It wasn't fair. But the kindness and concern were what was really setting my teeth on edge.

I didn't need her pity.

"Anyways," I blasted her with a bright, but dismissive smile, "I gotta go to the bathroom. So..." Enough said. I moved inside my stall, shut the door, and sat. Then I waited.

That was rude.

I was feeling like an asshole, but a moment later she was edging for the door. She was going slow, and that tugged at me because Taz Shaw wasn't known for moving at a slow pace. She bounced. She hurried. She darted. She didn't move slow, and she wasn't my friend.

The door swished open and closed, and I cursed under my breath.

But, what? Go and attend a rich asshole's party tonight as a tagalong? I wasn't a tagalong. I'd never been a tagalong, and fuck if I was going to become one.

But because my day was still in the toilet (lame humor), that didn't mean I couldn't mess someone else's day up, too.

I found the drugs, but I didn't hide them. I flushed them.

Then I went to my last detention of my high school career, and that sucked too.

I wished I hadn't flushed the drugs.

2

KESS

I was walking to the parking lot when I heard the bike's engine roar. A moment later, he parked on the clear opposite end of the lot, right next to my own motorbike. He did that on purpose. His head turned, his helmet still on, but I already knew the cockiest smirk of all smirks was on his face as he was watching me come toward him.

Christopher.

How I knew this guy was beyond me.

He transferred in the beginning of the year, and he was barely around. In fact, people really didn't know he was even at our school and I could get why. He showed up for first period, ducked out, and who knew where he disappeared to until seventh period.

I didn't know his story. I didn't know why he was only around for those two classes, how he got exempt from class projects, speeches, anything that might've drawn attention to him. But somehow it worked. The teachers never called his name for roll call. They literally skipped over him as if he wasn't in the classroom, and after a month of whispering from the girls and weird looks from the guys, they all accepted it.

It helped that he didn't say anything.

It also helped that he didn't linger after class. I'd never seen him talk to anyone. He showed up in the morning, went to class, left, and repeated the process at the end of the day. Did he have a locker? I hadn't a clue.

But I did know he was gorgeous.

Dark hair that he liked to run a hand through and pull on so the ends were a sexy mess. Then there was the square jawline. It always looked as if he'd done just a quick buzz over his jaw for the whiskers, and he let it go until the night again. And his face, nice and hella smoldering.

Seriously. It wasn't fair.

But he had the clearest blue eyes, and that's what gave him away. He didn't know I knew where he got those blue eyes, and that little fact kept my mouth shut. I didn't say one word about the secret I *did* know about Christopher Raith, besides his name and how him just waiting on his motorcycle gave off this intense pulse in the air.

He was sizzling.

He was also Red Demons royalty.

Red Demons. The fast-growing motorcycle club that was starting to take over not just California, but Nevada, New Mexico, Colorado, and all the way north from Montana to the south where rumors were circulating they were going to start moving into Texas.

Yes. This gossip I *did* listen to, mostly because my uncle was a Red Demon, and he'd stayed with my mom and me earlier in the year for a month. He hadn't said why he was here, but him showing up, then Christopher Raith popping up in class the next day seemed too much of a coincidence to not be connected.

My uncle never said a word, and I knew he wouldn't. He just grunted he was there on 'MC business' and that's all we got.

The other thing I knew was that Christopher knew I knew who he was.

But we'd never spoken a word to each other.
I was almost to my bike when he turned his engine off.
He stood up, and I stopped about ten feet back.
I guess the whole 'no talking' thing was about to end.

3

KESS

He sat back down on his bike, stretching his legs out. One hand rested on his thigh and the other on his handlebar. He was still wearing his helmet. He sat there, staring at me.

I stood there, staring back.

Neither said a word.

We were in a standoff, but yet we were speaking a whole lot. I was feeling the *vibes* in the air. They were strong, rippling back and forth between us, and my whole body was heated from the inside out. I felt feverish, and the strength it was taking to not break was a strain. A big strain.

I was going to break soon.

But, man. He had a helmet. That wasn't fair.

Finally, I flicked my eyes up. "Can I see your helmet?"

He stalled. I was guess that's not what he expected from me, but he reached up and took it off.

Goooood, those eyes. That face. That mouth.

I didn't have words. No guy who was MC royalty should be as pretty as him. A model, yes. Actor, yes. Even a punk preppy, and I had to admit, some of those looked decent. They weren't my cup of tea, but a girl could appreciate a nice face, nice physique, and what was promised to be a six-pack underneath a certain shirt.

My mouth was dry just wondering what was underneath his faded and ripped jeans, his riding boots, and his grey shirt shredded on the side. I saw it because his leather jacket was unzipped and hanging to the side.

He handed the helmet over, his face stony.

I took it, making sure our hands did not touch, and he noticed. The corner of his mouth lifted for a split second, then he went back to being a wall.

I didn't wait. I gathered my hair up and pulled the helmet down. When it was in place, I stood back, crossed my arms over my chest, and cocked my head to the side. Then I waited.

He frowned, his own head tilting to the side. "You trying to be funny?"

"Just wondering what it's like on this side of the helmet."

His eyes narrowed, those gorgeous blues, but he didn't say anything further.

Neither did I. That was the whole point of this.

After another few seconds, he shook his head slowly. "What are you doing?"

Maybe the gig was up, and it hadn't put him on edge. That'd been the hope.

I sighed, taking the helmet off, but I didn't hand it over. I held it, resting it just on the back of my thigh, and I nodded at his bike. "Since when do you guys wear these, anyway? I thought you needed open-face helmets?"

He leaned forward, plucking the helmet away from me, and moved back. "Easier for cameras not to spot me."

I looked at his bike's plate, but it was smudged over.

Who *was* this guy?

Fine. I'd try a different tactic, and what the tactic was for, I couldn't answer. I was going with it, feeling my way because there was a weird ebb and flow between him and me.

He probably wasn't here for me. Right?

I don't know.

He might've needed to hand something in, or... I had no clue, but my gut was telling me he was here for me. That he knew I had detention today. That he knew the exact time I'd be let out, and I'd even be let out early.

He had it all worked out to be here when I would be walking to my bike.

"What do you want?"

He didn't wait a beat. "You know me."

"Your name is Christopher Raith."

His eyes narrowed. "You know where I come from."

Now I shifted, rolling to the back of my heels. "I know whose blue eyes you inherited yours from, yes."

One nod from him. "He's my uncle."

His uncle was the president of the entire Red Demons MC. Max Raith.

Royalty.

I noted, "And you know my uncle."

A second nod. "I do."

Mine was not. He was a member, but I knew he was important to the original charter.

So I knew his uncle.

He knew my uncle.

We knew each other, but we didn't know each other, and still standing, staring, I knew we both wanted to *know* each other.

4

CHRISTOPHER

Kess Foster.

They never told me how gorgeous she was going to be, but she was. My dick had been hard for an entire year straight, and she was standing here, done with high school, and she never had a clue she'd been in danger.

'Club business.' That's what her uncle said he told her.

Club business, my ass. She had a right to know her life had been threatened and that she was the reason I was even here. All year. Her uncle was at the house until I got situated. We had a security system put in place, and I holed up close in the house next door. She never knew. Ever. When I rode my bike up, I went into the backyard. I asked Heckler, her uncle, if she wondered about the bike sounds. His response was she didn't. There were other bikes riding up and down their street but none of them were MC bikers.

I guess it worked.

As for the other reason *I* was here, I'd been the one chosen. A year older than her, I'd already graduated, and Max had been adamant I get my degree. Then this situation came up where there'd been rumors of someone trying to push in on a territory that wasn't quite ours, but we also didn't want to let anyone else in. Mix that with a few whispers that came down the pipeline one of ours had a niece in Roussou, California and how pretty her head might be as a trophy.

Max hadn't waited.

I got the order to head out immediately.

Word was worked out with local law enforcement. There were other players in town, a whole 'crew' system in the school so I hadn't needed to be around during the day. Not much. Not until the last semester. Things got dicey, and she had no clue, so I started hanging out a bit more than she realized.

But I was there, watching, and feeling like a creeper.

The threat was recently eliminated, so I got the call to head back to headquarters.

I waited, wanting to actually talk to her for once.

And I was back to this: Kess Foster. Beautiful and she was the kind that didn't know it. And what was more, she wasn't a common beauty; she was unique. Her hair was so blonde, it was almost white. It looked like she dyed it with some dark roots, but that was just her hair.

Heckler had the same hair, and it was weird.

If we were told that aliens came down and had been walking among us, I would've instantly thought Heckler and Kess were from them. That was in addition to their eyes. I had clear blue eyes. I knew this, and it was something I got a fuck-ton of attention from. They were my weapon. I could yield them how I wanted, but in her school, I kept my head down and my mouth shut. No one messed with me, but that was a testament to the school itself. The dynamics had been interesting here.

But my eyes weren't like hers.

Hers were an ice blue. Almost gray, almost just white too. I'd never seen eyes like hers.

One woman giggled over Heckler, saying his eyes were like a vanilla chai latte with a dash of light blue in them. Eerie.

But Kess didn't know.

She'd been in a crew, and those five guys had been protective of her. That was, until a storm went down and their crew disbanded. I watched it happen.

I watched as each guy left and were now already doing their own thing. One guy remained, but he'd shunned her, and I had no idea why.

She was alone, and she just graduated high school.

She shouldn't be alone.

This was the summer she was supposed to have a last hoorah with her friends before heading to college. That was one thing I *had* been proud of, because she was smart. She was going to school. Some in our life, my life, didn't do academic institutions. They were looked at as weapons for the 'other' way of life.

Max didn't view them that way, and I was glad that Heckler said his niece didn't either.

She was going to a fancy sounding school.

I was happy. I was proud.

She was smart. She was self-reliant. She wasn't a big fighter, but if push came to shove, she'd pick up a gun. She had good aim. I'd watched her at the gun range.

She'd be just fine, but she was alone, and I didn't like her being alone.

I also didn't like that she wasn't prepared for what kind of attention she was going to get moving forward. That made me worried, and my dick grew, calling me an asshole, because yeah, I was one of those guys.

I wanted to give her a whole bunch of attention.

5

KESS

He was still staring.

I hated to admit this, but it was just making me hotter and *more* bothered.

What was wrong with me?

I'd never been this girl. Ever. It's not that guys hadn't been interested, but once I joined my crew, those guys went away. There'd been a time I had dated one of my crew members, but it would've gone bad fast so that stopped immediately. After that, we'd been a no-dating crew. I loved my guys, or had loved them. They were my brothers. My family. We joined our freshman year, and our crew name had been Shane's Crew. Nothing fancy and named after Shane Lorenzo. He'd been our leader, but the rest of us all got along. There'd been problems, which was why I felt so blindsided.

They'd been my security blanket, and now, nothing.

Shane went to Alaska. Kemp and Gorrup were on their back-packing trip together. Johnny was still here, but not speaking to me. I had no clue why. And Curtis was probably face first in his girlfriend's pussy since we'd disbanded. She'd been eager for the end of us and now that it happened, I guess she was his new crew in the whole girlfriend/boyfriend thing.

Mostly we liked to drink beer and laugh together. We did pranks sometimes, mostly on teachers or the principal, or anyone who messed with us. But we weren't a fighting crew. We weren't known for that. We were just there in the background.

Christ.

They were me.

I was them.

That *was* me.

I was 'the background' and it was hitting me how stupid I'd been.

There had been conversations over the last year about the summer and next year. The guys had even said they were looking into going backpacking, but I thought they'd talk about it with the rest of us. And Shane had mentioned Alaska. I told them I was going to college. Johnny was doing the same.

But... just to disband? It hurt. It hurt a lot.

"Wanna get a burger?"

His gravelly voice pulled me out of my thoughts, and I tuned back in. His head had remained to the side, those eyes on me, piercing through me, and I was getting all flushed having different thoughts instead. Thoughts like something other than his eyes checking me out.

"Sure."

6

KESS

We went on his bike.

It was glorious.

It was freeing.

Barely any words all year, just the awareness of each other, and here I was, feeling like I was meant to be on the back of his bike. My hands were wrapped around his tight chest, my body against his, and I could feel his strength. This guy—whatever the real reason he'd been here—he'd not been a normal student. He just felt more.

He drove to a small burger café, backing his bike up at the front door. The place wasn't full, and I wasn't surprised. Everyone was partying and as I got off his bike first, handing him the helmet, his hand grazed mine.

A tingle shot up my arm, but I'd been tingling the entire ride.

I'd been like this since I saw him waiting for me.

It's a surreal feeling, your body taking charge and not letting your mind catch up. Because I *should* stop and question things, but the only question that came to my mind was why did it feel so right when he took my hand and led the way inside?

He shifted, walking behind me. A gentle hand on my back as

we took the booth in the far corner. No one was inside except the staff, but it was a small place. There were only five booths available.

I slid inside, and Chris sat next to me.

I raised an eyebrow, but his mouth twitched as he leaned around me to snag the menus. He slid one in front of me. "You need that?"

I pushed it aside. "I've lived in Roussou all my life, been here probably six dozen times."

He chuckled. "What are you getting then?"

"A deluxe cheeseburger with fries and a soda."

He nodded. "Maybe I'll have the same."

After we gave our orders, Chris seemed to relax beside me, but he wasn't. His entire side was pressed against mine, and I felt how tight he was.

"What's going on?" I waited until our drinks were served before asking.

He raised an eyebrow at me, picking his drink up and taking a sip. "What do you mean?"

"I know you're not going to tell me why you were really at my school, but you're tense. And you waited an entire year to approach me."

His eyes lit up. "You're cocky."

I grinned slowly. "Maybe. Maybe not."

He gave another dry chuckle. "Let's talk about you. You're going to college next year?"

I nodded and told him my plans. It was a good school, and I wanted to get a nursing degree. "My mom's a nurse. When my dad left, she was pregnant with me."

"You two are close?"

"Yeah."

"That's Heckler's sister, right?"

Whoa. He acknowledged knowing my uncle. "Yeah..."

He caught my reaction. "What?"

"Just," a shrug, "I never thought you'd talk about, you know."

I was getting flustered. I never got flustered. This was weird.

He laughed, noting my reaction. "What is this now?"

Why? Why now? Why today? Why at the end of the school year?

Screw it.

I tried to ignore how inflamed my face must have been. "Why were you at my school this year?"

His grin faltered; his voice got quiet. "I can't talk about that."

Okay. Another push. "Were you even a student?"

He was studying me, but then a reluctant shake of his head. "No. I wasn't, but your school's administration knew I was there and why I was there."

I sucked in my breath. That was huge. Huge! And what did it mean?

The food came, but neither of us moved to start eating.

He waited until the server had moved from hearing distance before saying, "Let's just say some people in high positions have a certain fear and debt to the MC."

And my last question. "Are you a member of the Red Demons?"

He wasn't as forthcoming, waiting a few beats before lounging back. His arm came up to rest behind me, and he moved so he was facing me. "That's a complicated answer."

"Why?"

MCs didn't like you asking questions about them, and certainly not someone who'd be Red Demon royalty. I was going for broke here.

I was holding my breath until I heard, "I graduated high school last year."

I was doing the math. "So, you would've prospected for the summer, then you were sent here?" That was a whole year, and most of it was spent away from his club.

"We'll see how it goes when I head back."

So, he *was* leaving.

My heart sank.

"Got it. Yeah."

He paused, then leaned forward. "Hey." His voice, so soft there.

It wasn't fair.

"Hey." Not as soft. He touched my shoulder, hooking his finger under my tank top strap. He moved it down, his finger balling it up.

Sensations were exploding down my body, inflaming every inch, and I was super aware of his body right next to me. So seriously aware. There was a whole throbbing situation starting, and that was making me all sorts of flushed.

"Look, I'm going to level with you."

That didn't sound good.

My throat was spasming as I waited, looking over and holding his gaze.

His eyes were all stormy looking, focusing on my lips before looking back up. "I asked for the day. I don't know what orders I'll get. I will probably get called back to headquarters, but I don't really know."

My tongue felt heavy. "So, you're saying you have the night?"

Regret flared over his face, tightening his expression. His eyes flared again in sympathy.

I hated that look.

"Yeah. I have tonight."

One night.

His finger started rubbing over my shoulder, moving under my strap. The food was long-forgotten, and he was watching me, waiting for something. I didn't know what, but did it really matter? One night. The rest of today.

This sucked.

I asked, my throat hoarse, "Why'd you wait all year?"

He cursed under his breath. "I couldn't."

I knew. I mean, I knew. That's how MCs were, especially if they sent a guy for a long-term mission. That meant he was someone. I already knew that, but he was so young and to be sent away for a nine-month assignment. Those didn't get handed out lightly. No matter who his uncle was, Chris was meant for big things with the Red Demons.

One night. Damn.

I knew my answer to what he hadn't asked.

"Got a place we can hang?"

His eyes dipped to my mouth. "Oh yeah."

7

KESS

"Really?"

I gaped at the house when he pulled into a driveway, then turned my head to the house next to it. My house. And I looked back to his house.

"You were my neighbor this whole time?"

A low chuckle reverberated from him as he turned the engine off and stood from his bike. "Yep."

I was even angrier, but one night. Dammit! I glared at him. "So not cool."

He ignored that, taking my helmet off and hanging it on his handle. He took my hand, giving me a tug. "Come on."

His eyes were wolfish. His gaze was lingering on my mouth, and just like that, the momentary anger was starting to subside. He hadn't even touched me.

Walking to the house, he lifted his arm around my shoulders. I reached up for his hand so they dangled together just off the side of me. This felt nice.

I was melting against his side.

Once inside, he stepped to the kitchen. "You want something to drink?"

You.

My throat went dry.

I croaked out, "No."

His eyes darkened, and he said softly, "Okay."

He took my hand again, leading me down the hallway.

Were we really going to do this? Was I really going to do this? Just get right down to business? I mean, he had bought me food, but yeah.

I was nervous.

I didn't date. It's not that I didn't want to, but there weren't a lot of guys I was interested in. I had a few hookups, but not many. A girl had needs. That was, until Christopher showed up. Once he did, it was him.

Only him. All him.

All year, and I was an idiot for not approaching him.

His room was sparse. A bed. A chair. A dresser. A laundry basket in the corner. That's all I noticed before he moved toward me.

One step.

He was right in front of me, close enough I could touch him.

Heat rose in me.

I was aching to touch him, and he was right there.

Another step.

His head folded down. His forehead rested on mine, and I reached out. My hands touched his stomach.

He was so strong, tight. There was no softness there, and both our chests rose at the same time.

I slid my hand up, pushing up his shirt, feeling the texture and contour of his muscles until I paused, right over his heart. It was speeding, just like mine, and biting down on my lip, I kept moving. His shirt was ripped off, his hand curling around my waist at the same time his head dipped.

His mouth found mine—and ooooh!

I was gone.

Done.

He was kissing me. I was kissing him.

I'd never been kissed like this.

He was commanding.

There was no soft, subtle seduction here. We both knew what we wanted. The whole year had been our foreplay, and his mouth opened over mine. I was helpless to do anything except respond. Hell, I was helpless to do *anything* except what my body wanted. And my body wanted a lot.

I wanted to crawl up him like he was a pole, and I wanted to feel him slide home.

Bending as his tongue swept against mine, he grabbed under my leg with one hand and his other hand on my ass. He lifted me. Oomph! He walked us backwards, lowering me gently onto the bed. He came down with me.

He moved down, his mouth trailing a path south until he lingered over my jeans.

He looked up, waiting.

I bit into my cheek and nodded. Yes, please. So many yeses.

My jeans were unbuckled, lowered, and his mouth moved there. He touched me, kissed me, and I lifted off the bed.

I was *inflamed*.

He explored me, every single inch of me.

He made me explode, then waited and brought me to the pinnacle again, and right before, he paused. A second. I heard the crinkle of a condom, and then he was back.

He had undressed me. I had done the same.

I relished in the feel of him, and then he moved between my legs. His eyes met mine, held me captive, and he slid inside.

So good. Sooo good.

As he began moving inside of me, and I was rolling with him, in the back of my mind, I knew it wasn't usually like this. There should've been clumsy fumbling. An awkward maneuver to unsnap my bra. I should've been embarrassed at how his fingers slid inside, and then gasped at how good that felt, but none of that happened.

The good part had happened, then happened again, and continued to happen, but this wasn't normal. We weren't normal.

He and I, we were made from the same fabric. It was *that* life, where I wasn't the cheerleader or the book nerd. He wasn't the jock or the frat preppy. He'd been born into a world outside the norm, and all my life, that's where I kept finding myself migrating toward.

Thrust.

Harder.

I wanted more.

Deeper.

Please.

Oh, *please.*

I didn't realize I was panting until he skimmed a hand up my throat, and his mouth leaned to capture mine once more.

God.

Yes. This was so out of the ordinary, but one night of this? It was better than no nights of nothing.

He groaned, pushing into me and holding there. "Come, baby. Come."

I didn't want to. I started to shake my head, trying to hold on, but then his hand dipped, and he found me right there. Oh-OH! I surged right over the edge, and I just kept right on going. My body was trembling, more waves were hitting me, and as he slid out and back in once more, I was clutching onto him, holding him to me.

One. More. Push.

He tensed, then I felt him jerking.

His body trembled just as mine had. He rested on me, a lazy kiss to my shoulder. "Fuck, woman." He grinned against my skin, moving to lay on his side.

I smiled, that same lazy feeling starting to course through me.

That was good. That was really good.

I said as much, trailing a hand up his arm and chest.

He lifted his head, dropping another kiss to my throat before finding my gaze. “Hell yeah, it was.” His words were raspy. His eyes were molten. They were on my mouth again, and his hand moved down between my legs. “*Jesus*. I could go again.”

“What?” I started to laugh, then was groaning as his mouth dipped down.

And he found me right where his fingers had been.

Oh, dear--oooooh.

I raked my hands through his hair and held on. I had a feeling the night had just started.

8

CHRISTOPHER

"Are you kidding me?"

The buzzing had woken me, and when I saw who was calling, I wanted to roll right back and pull Kess into my arms. We'd gone at it all night long. It'd been amazing, and now this?

I grabbed my phone and headed outside.

My uncle said, "I need you back."

I bit back a growl. "In the morning."

"Now. We're headed to Texas. I need you with me."

"In the morning."

"Now!"

He was our MC president, but he was my uncle.

Silence. Then, "What am I missing? You asked for a night to hang with friends—"

"Her. I wanted a night..."

"With Heckler's *niece*?"

He didn't sound happy about that. I gripped the phone tighter. "Yeah."

"Are you kidding me? Tell me this is a joke. Tell me I don't have to hang up, and when her uncle asks me what's going on, I don't have to choose to either lie to him or tell him the truth, that my nephew just banged his niece? Tell me I don't have to do any of that."

"She's not a one-night thing."

"What?"

I felt raw saying this, but to hell with it. "I held off all year. All year. I couldn't leave without—I protected her for nine months, Uncle Max. She's not a one-night thing."

There was more silence.

Another beat of it.

Then a gruff, "Well, that changes things."

I sighed, exhaling a little easier. "Does it change things enough?"

"Maybe. Let me make a few calls."

"Thank you, Uncle Max." I was about to hang up when he called my name again. "Yeah?"

"You did good this year. I'm proud of you."

My chest swelled up.

My uncle was the smartest and most dangerous man I knew. He could hire the killings of hundreds if he wanted. He had the men. He had the power. He had the connections, and he got there by being ruthless and brilliant at the same time. Words like that were not normal from him.

Yeah. My chest swelled up.

"Thank you."

"I'll be in touch. Go hold your girl again."

I hung up, turning to go back into the house, then stopped.

Kess was there, a bed sheet wrapped around her.

The moonlight was lit over her, casting half her body in shadows. I couldn't see her face or her eyes. I needed to see her eyes.

I began to move toward her, but she tightened her grip on the sheet in front of her and stepped forward. I saw her eyes.

I wished I almost hadn't.

Those eyes were fierce.
"You protected me for nine months?!"
Yeah. She *really* wasn't happy.

9

KESS

Nine months!

I'd been under threat for nine months, and from the little Chris said, I knew there was a whole ton more he wasn't saying.

There was a threat. He was young, so he'd been assigned to me. He watched me, and that was the gist of it. That was all he could tell me.

I wanted to rip him a new one, but I didn't want to harm him. Fillet him with my words, maybe, but not real filleting.

Nine months and I had no idea.

Its why Heckler came in the first place, and he'd been so vague when I asked why he was here.

"Just tell me who it was from?"

We were sitting in his living room. He was standing, leaning against the wall. I was on the edge of the couch, my elbows on my knees and my head in my hands.

"I can't. The rumors were higher up so we couldn't risk it. That's seriously all I can say."

I knew he couldn't, but it was driving me crazy.

In danger. Nine months. My mind couldn't wrap around that.

"That's why you moved next door."

He hesitated but nodded. "I installed a security system in your house. I could monitor you if something happened."

"And school?"

"Your crew wasn't in your first and seventh periods." He shrugged. "So I was."

He was right. They were in all my others. They were with me every other moment of the day, too. Lunch. After school. Except when I was home, and he was 'monitoring' me.

"How?"

He flinched at my tone. It was dull, grating.

He smoothed his hand through his hair. "I'd rather not tell you."

"Christopher!"

He flinched a second time.

Wait. I narrowed my eyes. "What's your club name?"

His jaw clenched. "Wraith."

Wraith.

I screwed a Wraith.

I didn't even want to know why he got that name.

"Oh my God!" I shoved to my feet, starting to pace. I slept with him, and I wanted to do it again. Who was I? I didn't even recognize myself with him. One meeting, our food unfinished, and we'd gone at it four times. Four. Times.

I couldn't. I just couldn't.

This was...this was ridiculous!

Heckler. My own uncle. I growled, "I'm going to murder my uncle."

Christopher or Wraith jumped in front of me, his hands up. "You can't. They can't know I told you. I don't—I might've gotten more time. I don't know, but if you call him, then that's all done for and I don't know what they'll want me to do next."

"Are you kidding me? You want more time?" I hissed.

"Well." He dropped his hands, frowning. "Yeah."

"Agh!" I screamed and shoved past him, going to his room and starting to dress.

"Babe."

"Don't!" I whipped back to him, one hand in the air and the other holding the sheet in front of me. "You are not my man or my boyfriend. You don't get to 'babe' me."

I dropped the sheet.

He groaned, raking his hand over his hair. "*Fuck*."

I grabbed my clothes, shoving my arms into my top and my legs into my jeans.

I didn't even remember where any of my stuff went

My phone.

My purse.

I stomped back to the front door,;there were my sandals. I didn't remember toeing them off, but I must've.

"Come on, Kess. Please."

I was so not listening to him.

Even if he was gorgeous...

And had protected me all year long...

Not happening.

Hell to the no.

But, oh man. How he felt in bed.

How he kissed me.

Slid inside of me.

He'd made me shatter in his arms, and not once or twice. Four times.

That was so not the norm.

I wrenched open the door—

His phone rang, peeling through the air.

I hesitated.

I hated that I hesitated.

He glanced down, then hit accept. "Max."

I froze.

On the other end of the phone was someone seriously powerful. It shouldn't have the power to impress me, but I couldn't help it. I was impressed, and I found myself waiting. I didn't know why. So yeah, I should go.

I was going.

Now.

Right now.

I was so going.

Damn. I was still here.

And I heard Chris saying, "I might have a situation here." A pause. "Okay. I'll take her."

He hung up, and now I really needed to go.

This time, I was going to do it. Go. Move forward.

Then he said, "Your friend Johnny..."

I frowned. "Yeah?"

He finished, "He's in trouble."

10

WRAITH

We went on my bike, heading out of Roussou toward Callyspo.

I didn't really know these guys well. They were a local charter in Frisco, but they asked to meet in Callyspo. There'd been a new setup put in charge. Things got messy a bit ago, so some restructuring was needed. That was before my uncle began to move south. When we rode in, I didn't stop and plan for Kess. Or for her reaction.

She was off the bike and across the lot, heading toward Johnny in a flash. "You're an asshole!"

One of the guys caught her, an arm wrapped around her waist. She had enough momentum so she was lifted in the air as her feet kept pedaling. She didn't care. She was seeing red.

Sauce came over, his jaw hard. "Couldn't leave your girl behind?"

"She's Heckler's niece."

He turned back. His eyes were now hard. "And you brought her *here*?"

Yeah. I knew.

I sighed, nodding at her ex-crew member. "So, he knew the old group?"

"Looks like. He approached us, said he had money and a party he could unload everything at four times the normal rate. Some rich kid in Fallen Crest."

"Is this relationship new?"

"With us, yes. We've never worked with him before. I'm assuming his usual supplier was pinched or dried up."

He was a potential problem. I didn't like potential problems.

Sauce went back to watching the show.

Johnny was trying to hide in the back of a cage, and Kess kept trying to get free from Rampant, her holder. Her nails were going into his arm, and I barked, "Kess! Hands off my guy."

Rampant shot me a grin as Kess lifted her hands away, but she went back to screaming at Johnny.

"And why'd you bring her again?"

I was asking myself the same thing. "What's the plan with him?"

"We were waiting for orders from your uncle. We're too new. Things are too delicate right now. We don't want to off someone, have it blow back on another charter, and we knew you were in town."

He was right. It could get back to me.

I was his age, in his school and the authorities already knew I was here.

Well. Damn.

Sauce read my expression and grunted. "Pretty much."

"What'd my uncle say?"

"He said to do what you decided."

I frowned. Why would he do that?

I nodded, taking my phone out. "I gotta make a call."

THAT CALL DIDN'T HELP.

"You clean it up how you want. Nothing can come back on us." That'd been his response, and I didn't like thinking I needed to be judge, executioner, and cleanup so early into my MC career. I thought I'd have a bit more time, but I *was* Maxwell Raith's nephew.

I was named Wraith for a reason too.

Shit.

Shit!

I was eyeing Kess, who had quieted. Rampant wasn't holding her anymore, but he and another were standing between her and Johnny.

This was my problem.

Johnny was her crew. That meant he'd had her back since they formed, and there was love there. Friendship love. Loyalty love. Family love. Love that was ride or die. But seeing him now, I knew he didn't feel the same. He was a weasel, and he was on the product. My guess was that he'd been doing it for a while, and so the love that Kess felt for him, not only did he not return it, but he didn't deserve it.

But he didn't have anything on us.

I walked over to him. "Who'd you work with before?"

He sneered at me. "Some pig."

Okay then. That helped with the decision.

I glanced back at Sauce. "Rough him up. Put him in the hospital for an extended stay, and you," I leaned down and got in his face, "if I get word you're dealing in Roussou, Fallen Crest, Frisco, or Callyspo, they will end you. Got it? I don't like you. You're a piece of shit."

His face was getting redder and redder. He opened his mouth —I shut it, with a fist.

He toppled out of the truck, and for good measure, he got a boot to the ribs. Then a second.

He lay there, moaning, but my message wasn't done.

"You don't seem to know what you are." I squatted down, my arms resting over my knee. "You're a future snitch."

He paled, his eyes then darting to the others.

"And what's worse, you're a junkie future snitch. Those types only die, so if you want to stay in town, you clean up. If you don't, these guys will relocate you, six feet under. Got it?"

His eyes went to Kess.

I growled, shifting to block his view. "And you *really* want to stay away from her. You go near her, you get me to deal with. You don't want to deal with me."

He didn't like it but he had no choice.

The guys hauled him out, given orders to drop him off in front of a hospital.

Kess went to wait by my bike, and I had another word with Sauce.

Then it was time to go back. I still had a few hours and I needed to make them memorable.

11

KESS

I was angry at Johnny, but I was more hurt.

It wasn't just him. I was hurt by our entire crew, because we weren't a crew. We'd just been pretending to be. And I was angry at myself for not figuring that out earlier than now. They all left, and they had gone quickly. I was hugging the back of Chris, and we were going back to his place. I didn't know when or even if I'd see him again. And yet, all of that aside, I felt like he was more crew than Johnny ever had been.

I pressed my forehead to Chris' back, tightening my arms.

He reached down, his hand running over my leg and then stayed there.

It felt nice. *Right.*

I would be sadder about when we'd have to say goodbye than my crew. That told me everything.

I was such a fool.

When we pulled back into his house, he led me by the hand, and we went back to his room.

We didn't sleep the rest of the night.

It was early. The clock said it was six in the morning when we'd collapsed after our last round.

I was resting half on his chest, drawing a circle over his stomach.

Both of us were sweaty and had no desire to move, not another inch. My body had no bones. I was a melting mess, and it was wonderful.

But still. The clenching in the stomach. It was there because his uncle was supposed to call. He'd shared that part when I asked when he needed to go, though I'd been dreading even speaking the words.

"Those guys are going to kill Johnny."

His body stiffened.

I lifted my head up. I wanted him to see that I knew. "I heard what you said to him, about doing drugs. You're right." Another thing I was kicking myself for not seeing. "I actually think I flushed his drugs today."

He moved his arm from behind his head and took my hand in his. Sliding his fingers through mine, he cocked his head to the side. "Good."

That note. I grinned, remembering it.

"What?"

I shook my head. "Nothing. There was a stupid note on the door. It was kinda funny." But thinking on it, "Johnny couldn't stash drugs in the girls' bathroom. Someone else must've done that."

Chris didn't respond, not that my statement even warranted a reply. It was done.

I sighed, laying my cheek back down on his chest. His free hand went through my hair, smoothing it down my back and up again. It was soothing and caressing at the same time.

"So, your uncle is going to call you to join their group?"

He tensed again.

I learned he did that anytime the Red Demons were brought up.

His voice was low. "Yeah. More than likely."

That meant I needed to deal with it, start getting over him.

Was it sad that I needed to get over a guy with whom I only had one night? Or maybe that was a beautiful thing?

I didn't know. Beautiful things didn't survive in my world.

I looked up.

That made sense too, because Chris was beautiful.

He looked down, his hand coming to cup the side of my face. "What's in your head?" His thumb ran over my cheek, so soft and tender. It matched his tone.

I wasn't going to tell him that, so I said something else, "Thank you for being here to protect me this year." My heart skipped a beat. "That's the nicest thing anyone's done for me."

"Oh, baby." He sat up, curling over me, and his mouth dropped to mine.

But there were no words that could be said.

He was going.

I was staying.

It was what it was.

We had the morning still.

Then his mouth was moving over mine, and before long, we'd shifted. I was straddling him, and his hands were on my hips.

The sun was spreading through the room, inch by inch, but I wasn't seeing it.

I was just feeling, and in a way, I felt like I was *feeling* for the first time.

12

CHRISTOPHER

My phone rang.

We'd both been waiting.

It was almost noon, so my uncle gave us half of another day. I wondered if that was part of his gift to me for handling the problem last night.

Taking my phone outside, I answered, "Hey."

"I have good and bad news. Which do you want?"

I sighed.

"The bad first."

Max chuckled low over the phone. "Pack up. I want your ass on your bike in thirty minutes. I'll send you the coordinates where to go."

I gripped my phone tight, hating this, hating everything about this.

"Okay." I was forcing air out through my nose, trying to keep my teeth from grinding. "And the good news?"

"Got a guy in the admissions office. Turns out, we need a college boy for our club. Guess where you're going to school?"

Wait.

"What?" I started to turn around.

Kess was sitting at the table, her knee pulled up. She was hugging her leg, and her head was cocked to the side. She was trying to figure out a puzzle in a magazine I had lying around. Jesus, she was stunning. A breeze was going through the room, and I was noticing every detail about how it was lifting some of her hair strands, making them wave in the air.

Goddamn romantic crap here.

My heartbeat was drumming thick in my ear.

There's no way I'd heard him right.

He laughed, though. "You heard me. You're coming here for three months, and then returning for your girl. Heckler told us where she's going to college. I need a future college degree guy in the club."

I swallowed. "What degree?"

"We'll get into that later. Go and break the news to your girl, and then get down here. Heckler's got something to say to you."

I was sure he did.

My uncle said thirty minutes, but he was going to have to wait.

I went and told Kess the news, and I didn't leave on my bike until later in the day.

Much, much later.

THE END

If you enjoyed Kess, please leave a review!
They truly help so much.
For more stories, go to: www.tijansbooks.com

ACKNOWLEDGMENTS

I'd like to thank the Bookworm Box because through their first anthology, I created Kess!

I also want to thank all the readers who love the Crew Series!

Thank you to the readers in my reader group, Tijan's Crew. Your constant support in there is so vital to me. Thank you, thank you, thank you!

ALSO BY TIJAN

Kess is written to be a short story, but if you'd like to read more about Taz and the Crew System from Roussou, check out:

Crew Series

Rich Prick (standalone)

Frisco

Other works in the same universe:

Fallen Crest/Roussou Universe

Fallen Crest Series

The Boy I Grew Up With (standalone)

Nate

Mafia Standalones:

Canary

Cole

Bennett Mafia

Canary

Jonah Bennett

Other series:

Broken and Screwed Series (YA/NA)

Jaded Series (YA/NA suspense)

Davy Harwood Series (paranormal)

Carter Reed Series (mafia)

The Insiders (trilogy)

Sports Romance Standalones:

Enemies

Teardrop Shot

Hate To Love You

The Not-Outcast

Young Adult Standalones:

Ryan's Bed

A Whole New Crowd

Brady Remington Landed Me in Jail

College Standalones:

Antistepbrother

Kian

Contemporary Romances:

Bad Boy Brody

Home Tears

Fighter

Rockstar Romance Standalone:

Sustain

Paranormal Standalone:

Evil

Micaela's Big Bad

More books to come!